I0819924

Pine Cone Academy: Hope vs Despair

Josh Zimmer

Welcome to Pine Cone Academy! Pine Cone Academy educates students of various talents to expand their knowledge of the world around them, and use their talents to solve various situations. A group of students walked on to the campus of Pine Cone Academy, with their heads held high for the future of their lives. The students walked in to the doors of Pine Cone Academy! The teachers prepared their classrooms for the new year of students, that were ready to expand their knowledge. The students were in the hallway, decorating their brand new lockers. Sally and Fiona walked through the hallway to the cafeteria. Pine Cone Academy hired them to serve lunch to all of the students. Even though their main goal was to serve lunch, Sally and Fiona had bigger plans for the school. Sally and Fiona's plans involved filling the school's hopeful environment with despair. The students filled their bags with their supplies, and walked to homeroom. The students walked in to the classroom, and sat down in their seats. The teacher was writing her name on the whiteboard. The teacher's name was Ash, and she is very cheerful and hopeful. One of the students put their feet on their desk. The student was Matt! Ash slammed her hands on the desk and yelled at him. Ash said, "No feet on the desk, the staff cleaned the desks earlier this morning." Matt growled and said, "Oh come on, I should be allowed to do whatever I want!" Ash threw a pair of scissors and said, "Don't argue with me, this isn't my first time dealing with troublemakers." Daniel smirked and said, "That's right hot shot, don't make the teacher angry!" Ash said, "No words from you either, Daniel!" Anha said, "Listen to the teacher, pipsqueak!" Matt said, "Shut Up Anha!" Anha and Matt got up from their desks. Tony got up from his desk

and said, "Anha calm down, it's the first day of school." Anha said, "Making drama is my specialty." Tony sat down at his desk. Steve said, "Tony, it will be fine, Anha needs to handle this on her own." Tony nods and watches the chaos between Matt and Anha. Matt tackles Anha in to the wall! Anha backflipped and kicked Matt in the face. Matt punched Anha in the face. Anha punched Matt in the face. Matt slid backwards and took out his knife. Anha took out her knife and sped towards Matt. Matt swung his knife at Anha. Anha swung her knife at Matt. Matt kicked Anha in the chest. Anha flinched and slid backwards. Matt grabbed Anha by the neck and choked her. Anha put her hand on Matt's neck and choked him. Anha body slammed Matt in to the ground. Matt got up and sweeped his leg under Anha. Anha fell on the ground! Anha got up from the ground, and roundhouse kicked Matt in the chest!

Matt smashed in to the wall! Matt growled, as he got up from the ground. Anha growled at Matt! Ash threw her coffee mug at Matt. The coffee mug hit Matt in the chest, splashing coffee all over his clothes and the floor. Ash said, "That is enough, all of your talents would go to waste if you guys killed each other in my classroom. Matt and Anha, as your punishment, you will be cleaning my classroom." Anha said, "I hate cleaning so much!" Ash said, "No arguments allowed, I am strict, and when you interrupt the flow of my classroom, you will be punished! Both of you sit down, or I will chain you to your desks!" Matt and Anha got terrified in fear and sat down at their desks! The bell rings in the background! Ash said, "Have fun in your classes, students!" Steve put his science notebook, and the rest of his supplies in to his bag. Steve got up from his seat and walked out of the classroom! The rest of

the students got up from their seats and walked out of the classroom. Steve and Daniel walked through the hallway together. Steve said, "I wish Anha would cool down, getting in fights with the other students would affect her future." Daniel said, "I agree, but she probably had a bad experience during her life." Steve said, "Her lifestyle is different than us, she probably got her behavior from her parents." Daniel said, "Makes sense, I feel bad for the homeroom teacher." Steve said, "The homeroom teacher was very nice and hopeful!" Steve and Daniel walked by Peter's locker! Peter was at his locker, putting supplies in to his bag. Daniel said, "Hey Peter, how is it going?" Peter said, "I am doing good so far, I am ready for the Algebra class." Daniel said, "That's good, positivity and optimism are needed to succeed in life." Peter, Steve, and Daniel walked in the hallway together to Algebra class. Anha and Tony were

walking in the hallway together. Tony said, "Why do you have to make drama, everywhere you go? It frustrates the other students around you." Anha said, "It is part of my talent!" Anha and Tony walked to Algebra class! Anha and Tony walked in to the classroom for Algebra. Anha sat down at her desk. The other students walked in to the classroom and sat down at their desks. Peter and Steve were at their desk, getting their supplies out of their bags. Daniel was at his desk, getting supplies out of his bag. Tony's desk was next to Daniel's desk. Tony sat down at his desk! Tony got his supplies out of his bag, ready to take down any Math equations that were thrown at him. James walked to the whiteboard, and wrote on it. James said, "Welcome to Algebra, students! Some of you know me as the student council president, and I am also your Algebra teacher for the current school year at Pine Cone Academy! Today

is the first day of school for everyone, and I have a special surprise." James took out a stack of exam papers and put them on his desk. James said, "This is a surprise exam, do your best everyone! The staff of Pine Cone Academy are counting on all of you to do well." Peter said, "Surprise Exam, with my luck, I can take down every Math equation and pass!" Steve said, "Math exams are a piece of cake, I bet that I will do well." Daniel panics and flips through his notebook. Daniel rubs his hand through his hair and said, "Surprise Exam, but I didn't study! What if I fail, and my entire academic career falls apart? My family members will kill me, if I don't get passing grades in all of my classes." Tony put his hand on Daniel's arm and said, "Daniel, everything will be ok, you are the smartest person that I know. Your optimism has helped me and everyone else survive the world around them." Daniel smiled at Tony and said, "Thanks

buddy for the support!" Tony said, "No problem, lets take down the Math equations together." Chris said, "Daniel, you're the smartest person that I know, and you will destroy the Math equations on the exam." Daniel said, "Thanks for the support, Chris!" Chris said, "I am a good motivator for everyone." Tony said, "Chris, I hope you do well on the Math exam as well." Chris said, "Thanks Tony, you're the best!" Anha said, "Shut up, plants are boring to look at, and their pollen messes up my hair, by landing on my head." Tony said, "Plants are awesome to look at, you can admire the beauty of them, by examining the details of the flowers on them." Anha said, "Seems boring, I don't like nature, it annoys me so much." Tony said, "Just because you don't like nature doesn't mean that you can insult plants." James said, "Both of you quiet down! Save the energy and motivation for the Math

equations on the exam." James walked around the classroom and put the exam on everyone's desk. James said, "The exam starts now, and you have until the bell rings to finish the exam and put it on my desk. Good luck everyone!" The students knocked out the Math equations on their exams. Daniel moved his hand through his hair, as he finished the Math equations on his exam. Daniel set his pencil down, and got up from his desk. Daniel walked up to the teacher's desk and turned in his exam. Tony followed behind Daniel and turned in his exam. Steve and Peter turned in their exam! Tony and Daniel put the pencils in their bags, as the other students turned in their exams. The bell rings in the background. Steve and Peter put their supplies back in to their bags and zipped them up! Daniel said, "Oh boy, time went by so fast!" Tony winks and said, "Yep, time goes by fast, when you have fun taking down Math

equations." Steve and Peter got up from their seats and walked in to the hallway! The other students got up from their seats and walked in to the hallway. Daniel and Tony walked in to the hallway together. Daniel and Tony walked in to the library and sat down at the table. Steve and Bob were sitting next to them, laughing while reading science jokes out of a joke book. Matt was sitting at the table next to them, reading a history book about technology. In the corner of the library, Noah and Monica were hanging out together, eating popcorn. Noah and Monica smiled at each other! Noah said, "Monica, you have been a wonderful friend, since we have met each other." Monica said, "Noah, you have been a wonderful friend as well. I hope nothing breaks our friendship." Noah and Monica hug each other. Noah and Monica rehydrated themselves, by drinking out of their water bottles. Noah and Monica took

out their notebooks and studied for their classes. In the computer lab, Joey and Abby were playing a action role playing game called Dragon Slayers on the computer. Joey said, "Abby, distract the dragon by shooting your fire spell at his head, and I will jump on his head and stab him with my sword." Abby said, "Sounds good, be careful, we don't have alot of health potions left." The dragon roared and walked towards Abby's character. Abby shot her fire spell at the dragon's chest. The dragon growled and chased after Abby, as her character ran in to the forest. Joey jumped through the trees, and chased after the dragon. Joey took out his sword, and flipped out of the tree. Joey jumped on to the dragon's back, and used his sword to help him climb. The dragon swished his tail at Abby! Joey kept his balance on the dragon's back, as he climbed towards the head. Abby ran in to a rock wall, as the dragon got closer to

her. The dragon sharpened his fangs and growled at Abby. Joey climbed on to the dragon's head! Joey flipped in the air, and stabbed his sword in to the dragon's head. The dragon roared in pain, as Joey flipped in the air and landed in front of Abby. Abby and Joey high fived and hugged each other, as they celebrated their victory in the computer lab. Joey and Abby saved their game progress on the computer. In the game room, Quentin, Sam, and Peter were playing Monopoly at the table. Quentin was in control of the dark blue properties, and Peter was in control of the red properties. The dark blue properties and the red properties had hotels on them. Sam rolled the dice and moved his game piece. Sam landed on one of the dark blue properties. Quentin smiled and said, "The property rent is $1000!" Sam gave the Monopoly money to Quentin. Sam said, "My Monopoly money is low, I need to be careful." Quentin rolled the dice and moved his game piece. Peter rolled the dice and moved his game piece. Sam rolled the dice and moved his game piece. Sam's game piece landed on one of the red properties. Peter said, "The property rent is $2000! Sam gave the Monopoly money to Peter. Quentin smiled and said, "One more property rent, until Sam goes bankrupt, and we get all of his Monopoly money." Quentin rolled the dice, and moved his game piece. Peter rolled the dice, and moved his game piece. Sam rolled the dice, and moved his game piece. The game piece landed on the dark blue property. Quentin said, "The property rent is $3000!" Sam looked down at his small pile of Monopoly money, and noticed that he doesn't have enough Monopoly money to pay Quentin. Sam sighed and gave the rest of his money to Quentin. Quentin smiled and high fived Peter! Sam broke down in tears, and put his head down in his hands. Sam said,

"My luck has failed me, I went bankrupt during a game of Monopoly." Sam sat in the corner, while Quentin and Peter cleaned up and put the Monopoly game away. Jay walked over and sat next to Sam. Jay said, "What's wrong, Sam?" Sam dried up his tears and said, "Peter and Quentin made me go bankrupt in Monopoly." Jay said, "It's just a board game, going bankrupt isn't the end of the world. They were just following the rules and playing fairly." Sam smiled and said, "Thanks for comforting me, Jay, you're an wonderful friend." Sam and Jay hug each other! Jay said, "It's getting close to lunch time, want to walk to the cafeteria with me?" Sam said, "I would love to!" Sam and Jay walked to the cafeteria! The bell rings in the background! Daniel and Tony walked out of the library, and toward the cafeteria. The other students walked out of the library, toward the cafeteria. Sam and Jay were walking

toward the cafeteria, when multiple students ran past them. Jay yelled at them and said, "No running in the hallways!" The students ignored Jay and continued running toward the cafeteria. Jay sighed and said, "Students these days don't know the rules of walking in the hallways." Sam said, "It's fine, they probably wanted to get to the food before it got cold." Jay and Sam walked by Ash's classroom! Sam said, "I wonder how Anha and Matt are handling their punishment with Ash." Jay said, "I bet that they are having fun handling their punishment." Jay and Sam walked in to the cafeteria. Ash tied a chain to Matt and Anha's neck. Anha said, "Why did you tie a chain to our neck?" Ash said, "The chain is to help me torture you guys during your punishment. It wouldn't be fun, if you guys tried to escape." Matt said, "Tying a chain to our neck is insane, we are just students." Ash laughed and said, "You guys interrupted

the atmosphere of my classroom. As your homeroom teacher, you need to learn respect and teamwork." Anha said, "This is unfair, students shouldn't be tortured for the teacher's entertainment." Ash pulled on the chain and dragged Anha to her. Ash said, "Life isn't fair, deal with it!" Ash gave a mop and a bucket of water to Anha and Matt. Ash said, "Clean the classroom, and exterminate all of the dust." Anha and Matt grabbed the mop and the bucket of water, and they started cleaning the classroom. Anha is cleaning with her mop, and sighs to herself. Anha looks at the clock and said, "This will take forever!" Anha picks up the bucket, and poured the water on to the ground in a huge area. The water poured out of the bucket and splashed everywhere. The water splashed on Ash's desk, and Matt's clothes. Matt growled and grabbed Anha's shirt. Matt shouted and said, "You ruined my clothes, and now I am soaking wet."

Matt kicked Anha in the chest. Anha stumbled backward and ran in to the desk. Matt grabbed Anha by her neck, and threw her in to the bookshelf. The books fell on top of Anha. Anha growled, as she got up from the ground. Anha sped in to Matt, and punched him in the face. Matt growled, as he slid backwards. Matt sped in to Anha, and body slammed her in to the desk. Matt held Anha on to the desk, and held her arms behind her back. Anha screamed in pain! Matt growled and said, "Say Uncle!" Anha said, "I will not say it to a crazy psycho like you!" Matt smiled and said, "Oh well, here is a little reward for entertaining me!" Matt took out his knife and cut off some of Anha's hair. Some pieces of Anha's hair fell on the ground! Anha screamed in horror and said, "My hair is ruined!" Matt smirked and said, "Your new hair cut matches you perfectly!" Matt tossed his knife in the air, and caught it. Anha and Matt refilled the

bucket of water and continued cleaning the classroom. Ash said, "Let's torture you guys a bit!" Ash pulled on the chains and spins them in a circle. Anha and Matt spin in a circle. They tripped on the bucket of water, and they fell on to the ground. Anha rubbed her back with her hand, as Matt grabbed the desk with his hand. Ash pulled on the chain, as Matt rolled on the ground, and ran in to Anha. Anha is on top of Matt, as Anha stares in to Matt's eyes and smiled. Matt threw Anha on to the ground, as he gets up. Matt brushes the dirt off of his clothes. Anha gets up, and brushes the dirt off of her clothes. Ash walks over to Anha and Matt, and unlatches the chains off of their necks. Matt and Anha walked out of the classroom, and to the cafeteria. Sally and Fiona walked past Matt and Anha! Sally and Fiona put their lunch gowns on. Sally said, "Serving lunch to these hopeful students is despairful!" Fiona said, "It could be fun!" Sally laughed and said, "You think serving lunch is fun, your head is filled with marbles. Pine Cone Academy is filled with hope and friendship!" Fiona said, "Do you have a plan to tear down the wall of hope?" Sally took out a flash drive and said, "With this flash drive, it lets us upload the Despair video in to any device, and brainwash the students to do whatever we want." Fiona said, "The plan is perfect, this is why you're so awesome, Sally." Sally and Fiona laughed maniacally together, as they walked in to the cafeteria. Students walked in to the cafeteria, as Sally and Fiona stirred the food in their cooking pots. The students lined up to get the food poured on to their lunch trays. Noah and Monica were standing next to each other with their lunch trays. Noah said to Sally and Fiona, "Give us a lunch that is perfect for friends to eat together." Noah winks at Monica, as Sally and Fiona poured the food on to

the trays. Monica and Noah smiled at each other, as they walked to the lunch table with their food. The other students got their lunch poured on to their trays, and they sat at the tables to eat their food. Tom and Victoria were sitting together, eating their food. Tom was rubbing his hand through Victoria's hair, as he ate his lunch. Victoria said "Tom, do you like rabbits?" Tom said, "Rabbits are cute and cuddly, and they have soft fur." Victoria ruffles up Tom's hair and said, "Rabbits are one of the greatest wonders of the world." Tom said, "This is why you're a wonderful friend, Victoria! You entertain me with wonderful stories." Victoria blushes, as she continued to eat her food. Jay and Sam were at the lunch table with Tom and Victoria, eating their food. Jay said, "The food is ok, but I expected better effort from a high quality school." Sam said, "The food satisfies my hunger, it is better than eating nothing."

Jay said, "You're right, Sam, eating nothing would fill us with despair." Noah and Monica were eating their food next to Sam and Jay. Noah smiled at Monica! Noah said, "What soap did you use in your hair, it smells nice?" Monica said, "I used strawberry soap to wash my hair." Noah said, "Strawberries are my favorite fruit to eat." Monica said, "Strawberries are amazing!" Noah winks and said, "I agree, you are amazing as well." Monica blushes, while she eats her food. Noah and Monica hugged each other! Noah and Monica got up from the table, and threw their lunch trays away. Noah and Monica went back to the table, and sat next to Sam and Jay. The students continued eating their food, as Sally and Fiona activated their cleaning robot. The cleaning robot was named the Cleaning Master 500! The Cleaning Master 500 rolled on to the cafeteria floor. Tom was walking to the trash can, and he tripped

on the Cleaning Master 500! Tom fell on the floor! Tom's plate of food flew in the air and landed on Daniel's shirt. Daniel growled as he wiped the food off of his shirt. Daniel got up from his seat, and picked up a pizza slice from the selection of food at the food bar. Daniel threw the pizza slice at Tom! The pizza slice landed on Tom's shirt. Tony shouted and said, "Food Fight!", as he threw a plate of meatballs at Gwen and his soda at Bob. Chris threw a egg roll at Victoria! The egg roll exploded, as it hit Victoria's chest. Tom and Victoria threw lettuce at Chris. The lettuce hit Chris in the face. Chris threw a bowl of soup at Norman. The bowl of soup landed on Norman's shirt. Norman threw burritos at Joey and Abby. The burritos hit Joey and Abby in the chest! Joey and Abby threw a cake at Quentin and Peter. The cake hit Quentin and Peter in the chest. Quentin and Peter picked up a tub of ice cream, and poured it on Daniel's head. Quentin and Peter continued pouring ice cream all over Daniel. Quentin and Peter picked up a bottle of salsa and nachos from the food bar and threw it at Joey and Abby. The bottle of salsa landed in Joey's hair, and poured all over his body. The nachos exploded all over Abby's body. Harry threw a bottle of ketchup at Norman. The ketchup exploded all over Norman's hair. Norman tackled Harry in to the cheese dispenser. The cheese dispenser poured cheese sauce on Harry. The cheese sauce landed in Harry's hair and covered his clothes, as the dispenser continued pouring the sauce on to him. Steve picked up a pot of chili, and poured it on Harry and Norman. Sam poured his chocolate milk shake on Jay. Jay poured orange juice on Sam. Matt and Anha threw a cake at Jay and Sam. Tony poured a gallon of chocolate sauce on Steve. The chocolate sauce covered Steve's body!

Joey and Daniel poured a gallon of ice cream on Quentin and Peter. Eddie walks in to the cafeteria and saw all of the chaos, as the students threw food everywhere. Eddie picked up a megaphone and shouted, "Drop the food now!" A breeze of cold air flowed through the cafeteria, as the students dropped the food on to the ground. Eddie said, "Students, clean yourselves outside. The cleaning robot will clean the cafeteria." The students walked outside and cleaned themselves. Multiple cleaning robots cleaned the food in the cafeteria. Sally and Fiona walked out of the cafeteria. Sally and Fiona walked through the hallway! Sally said, "The best way to spread despair is to get rid of the teachers. The students will fall apart, when their mentors can't teach them anymore." Fiona said, "That sounds like a awesome idea, Sally!" Sally and Fiona walked to the teacher's lounge! Sally opens the door, and walks in to the room. Fiona took explosives out of her bag and attaches them to everything in the teacher's lounge. Fiona connects the explosives to her detonator! Ash tapped Fiona on the shoulder and said, "What are you doing here?" Fiona said, "The teacher's lounge needed a makeover!" Ash said, "Oh ok, the teacher's lounge needed a makeover for a while." James came in and said, "The students are probably worried about us, lets head back to the classroom." Ash said, "They can handle themselves on their own." Sally said, "That's right, stay in the teacher's lounge, the students are fine on their own." Sally and Fiona smiled, as they pressed the button on the detonator. The explosives started to beep in the background. Sally said, "We love to hang out, but we are needed in another part of the school." Sally and Fiona walked out of the teacher's lounge. The explosives detonated, and the teacher's lounge exploded in the background. The bodies of Ash and James laid on the ground in puddles of blood. Sally and Fiona laughed maniacally, while they walked down the hallway. The students walked back in to the school. Steve walked to the water fountain and rehydrated himself with some water. Sally and Fiona walked in to the art room. Norman was sitting at the table, drawing in his notebook. Commander Fluff, Norman's teddy bear, was sitting next to him as his bodyguard. A cold breeze flowed through the room as Sally and Fiona walked closer to Norman. Norman was drawing in his notebook. Sally tapped Norman on the shoulder. Norman got spooked by Sally, and fell out of the chair. Sally said, "I am sorry, that I have spooked you!" Norman got up and brushed the dirt off of his clothes. Sally said, "What were you drawing?" Norman said, "I was drawing dragons in my

notebook! I want to make people smile with my drawings." Sally said, "Drawings are a wonderful way to express your imagination." Fiona picks up Commander Fluff and squeezes him. Norman said, "Don't hurt Commander Fluff, he is my friend and he helps me survive." Sally puts a knife at Commander Fluff's chest. Sally said, "Commander Fluff's life is on the line! He is about to lay on the ground in a pile of fluff." Norman trembles in fear! Norman puts his finger on his chin, as he thinks to himself. Norman mutters to himself as he said, "Commander Fluff is going to get the stuffing knocked out of him!" Norman tackles Sally in to the wall. Sally kicked Norman in the chest. Norman slid backwards. Sally laughed and said, "Execution Time!" Norman trembles in fear, as Sally laughed. Sally stabbed the knife through Commander Fluff's chest. Sally tears Commander Fluff's head off of his body. Sally threw Commander Fluff on

to the ground, as stuffing poured out of him. Norman laid against the wall, and cried in his shirt sleeve. Sally said, "Despair is so delicious, as it flows through the school!" Norman wiped the tears away, as he got up. Sally rubs her fingers on Norman's neck! Sally said, "Every decision that a human makes has a consequence! Despair will take over and squeeze all the hope out of the school like a python." Sally puts her knife at Norman's neck. Norman was shaking in fear as he said, "I don't want to die, I have so much hope to spread with my drawings." Sally said, "Awwwww, the kiddo has a talent that he likes to share with the world to spread hope." Steve walks in to the art room, and threw his science notebook at Sally. The science notebook knocked the knife out of Sally's hand. Steve kicked the knife across the room, as he said "Get away from him!" Steve tackled Sally in to the wall. Fiona

sneaks up on Steve with her knife. Steve grabbed Fiona's arm and flipped her on to the ground. Norman grabbed his notebook and walked in to the art closet. Sally kicked Steve in to the bookshelf. Steve laid against the bookshelf, as Sally swung her knife at him. Steve kicked Sally in the chest. Sally flinches, as she gripped her knife. Fiona got up from the ground, and stabbed Steve in the arm with her knife. Steve grabbed Fiona's arm, and threw her at the wall. Fiona laid against the wall. Sally tackled Steve in to the ground, and stabbed him in the back with her knife. Blood leaked on to the ground, as Steve laid on the ground. Fiona got up, and regained her balance. Fiona stepped on Steve's back to hold him down on the ground. Sally stabbed her knife in to Steve's neck. Blood poured out of Steve's neck! Steve grabbed on to a paint bottle with his arm, and hits Sally in the chest. Sally flinched, as she slid backwards.

Steve got up from the ground, and roundhouse kicked Sally in the face. Sally sped into Steve, and grabbed him by the neck. Sally smashed Steve in to the art table. The art table snapped in half, as Steve laid on the ground. Blood leaked out of Steve's body. Fiona picked up Steve, and held him against the wall! Sally stabbed her knife in to Steve's chest. Blood splashed on to the ground, as Sally picked up Steve, and threw him on the ground. Steve laid on the ground, in a puddle of blood. Eddie and Twilight kicked down the door to the art room. Eddie shot a tranquilizer dart at Sally and Fiona. Sally and Fiona laid against the wall. Twilight walked to Steve's body, and attached her medical equipment to his arm. Twilight signaled Eddie to come closer to her. Eddie said, "Is everything ok?" Twilight said, "I checked his pulse, and I didn't get a signal from the equipment." Eddie said, "Is that a good sign or a bad sign?" Twilight said, "It is a bad sign! When the equipment doesn't get a signal, it means that they are dead." Eddie said, "We need to clean up the mess!" Twilight nods, as she puts her equipment away. Norman walked out of the art closet, and saw all of the blood. He trembled in fear, as he walked through the room. Norman saw Steve's body, and screamed in horror! Norman broke down in tears, and cried on Eddie's shirt. Eddie said, "Norman, everything will be fine!" Norman cried and said, "I lost two of my friends, the world is falling apart!" Eddie said, "I know, life is rough right now, but we will bring justice to Sally and Fiona." Twilight wrapped a towel around Steve's body! Twilight picked up Steve's body, and carried him outside with Norman. Eddie used the cleaning robot to clean up the blood in the art room. Twilight and Norman walked in to the gardening shed. Norman picked up a shovel from the

gardening shed, and dug a hole for Steve's body. Twilight dropped Steve's body in to the hole. Norman filled up the hole with dirt. Norman put the shovel back in to the gardening shed. Sally and Fiona pulled the tranquilizer dart off of their chest, and walked out of the art room. Sally and Fiona walked to the headmaster's office! Fiona kicked the door open! Sally walked in to the headmaster's office, and set up the conveyor belt with the shotput ball. Sally wrapped the rope around the lights, as it hanged in front of the room, waiting for its prey. Fiona set up the spiked trap in front of the door. Eddie walked in to the headmaster's office, while Sally sat in the headmaster's chair. Eddie walked on to the spiked trap. The spiked trap activated, and Eddie limped in to the rope. The rope wrapped under Eddie's legs, and pulled him in to the air. Sally smiled and said, "You fell in to our trap,

headmaster. The storm of despair flows through the school, and it will devour the students, and smash their hope to pieces." Eddie said, "Hope will find a way to push back the despair." Sally smiled, as she gripped the knife in her hand. Sally threw her knife at the rope. The rope snaps, and the conveyor belt with the shotput ball activates. Eddie landed on the ground! The shotput ball fell on top of Eddie's head, and smashed his skull. Blood poured on to the ground, as Eddie laid on the ground. Sally picked up her knife from the ground, while Fiona picked up the rope. Fiona took down the conveyor belt and put the shotput ball in to her bag. Sally sat in the headmaster's chair, and loaded up the security system for the school. The computer beeped and said, "Put in the password to continue!" Sally taps on the keyboard and typed in a random combination of letters. The computer beeped and said, "Login

successful!" Sally tapped on the security camera system with the mouse, and loaded it on to the computer. The security camera system popped up on the screen, with camera footage of every location in the school. Sally smiled, as she tapped on to the upload button with the mouse. Fiona watched Sally, as she flipped her knife in the air. Sally plugs the flash drive in to the computer. Sally uploaded the Despair video in to the security camera system. Sally plugged the headmaster's microphone in to the computer, and turned it on. Sally said, "Time for the fun to begin!" Fiona said, "I can't wait to see the students suffer." Several students were hanging out in the hallway. Harry and Bob were chugging down a tub of ice cream, while Gwen was watching them. Harry and Bob put their hands on their head as they said, "Ahhhhhhhhhh, Brain Freeze!" Gwen facepalms and said, "You guys are idiots!" Harry and Bob said,

"Even though, we are idiots, it is fun to chug down ice cream, and get a brain freeze." Harry gave Gwen bunny ears with his fingers, while Bob took their photo with the phone. Harry and Gwen looked at the photo. Harry said, "Wow, the photo looks awesome." Gwen tickled Harry! Harry rolled on the floor, laughing! Bob tickled Gwen! Gwen was on the floor, laughing with Harry! Daniel and Tony did a headstand next to the wall. Noah and Monica reenact Sherlock Holmes to each other. Joey shared a bag of pretzels with Abby. Joey said, "I was playing Robot Warriors, and my character was battling a lion. My character defeated the lion with a spinning roundhouse kick, and stabbed it in the chest with his flaming sword." Abby said, "That is cool, Robot Warriors is one of my favorite games." Abby ruffles up Joey's hair! Joey smiled at Abby, while he eats a pretzel. Quentin and Peter have a dancing competition against each other. Peter does the robot, and Quentin does the moon walk. Peter said, "Hey Quentin, I dare you to do a backflip and impress the other students." Quentin agrees to the challenge by shaking his hand with Peter. Quentin backflips in the air, spins in a circle, and lands on the ground in front of the other students. Joey smiled and gave Quentin a pretzel. Joey hugged Quentin and said, "That was amazing, Quentin!" Quentin smiled and hugged Joey back! Sally pressed a button on the computer in the headmaster's office. The TV monitors in the hallways flipped on, with a video of despair. Sally's voice echoed through the hallways as she said, "Hello kiddos, we have a wonderful video to share with you today! Enjoy the despair!" The video played on the monitors!" A group of students followed Sam and Jay in to the janitor's closet. Peter and Daniel said, "Blind your eyes, don't watch the video!" Another group of students followed Peter and Daniel in to the men's bathroom. Tony grabbed Anha's hand, and locked himself in his locker with her. Matt was drinking out of the water fountain, and looked at the video monitor. Sally pressed a button, and a electric chain popped out of the monitor. The electric chain latches on to Matt's neck. The electric chain electrocutes Matt, as the energy flows through him. Matt's eyes turned red, as he gets consumed with despair. Sally smiled, as Matt flipped his knife in the air. Sally said, "Time to hunt down some students!" Matt walked toward the lockers, with his eyes glowing red. He walked over to Tony's locker and saw Tony terrified in fear with Anha. Matt cuts a hole in to the locker with his knife, and pulled it open. Tony is terrified and shaking, while Matt smiled at him. Matt grabbed Anha's arm! Tony grabbed Anha's arm, and pulled her back. Matt kicked Tony in the chest. Tony loses his grip on Anha's arm. Matt pulled harder on Anha's arm. Matt pulled Anha in to the hallway. Anha stumbled backwards! Matt kicked Anha in the chest. Anha leans against the wall! Matt picked up Anha by her neck, and slams her in to the locker. Anha laid against the locker, with blood leaking from her arm. Matt took out his knife, and sped towards Anha. Anha grabbed Matt's arm and roundhouse kicked him in the chest. Matt flew in to the wall, with his knife falling on to the ground. Matt got up from the ground, and picked up his knife. Anha punched Matt in the face. Matt fell backwards, and growled at Anha. Matt stabbed Anha in the chest with his knife. Blood leaked on to the ground, as Anha fell backwards. Matt tackled Anha in to the locker! Matt stabbed his knife in to Anha's neck, and punched her in the face. Anha fell backwards, and leaned against the wall! Matt picked Anha up by her neck, and threw her on to the ground. Matt stepped on Anha's back, and punched her in the face. Matt stabbed Anha in the back with his knife. A puddle of blood formed under Anha's body, as she laid on the ground. Matt flipped his knife in the air, as he smiled and walked to the next locker. Tony looked outside the locker, and saw Anha's body. Tony is terrified in his locker, while crying in his shirt sleeve. Daniel and Norman looked outside the men's bathroom and saw Anha's body. They were horrified, as despair filled the hallway with Matt patrolling outside. Norman sunk down, laid against the wall and cried. Peter and Daniel comforted Norman and wiped away his tears. Peter said, "Everything will be fine, despair will not win." Norman said, "It feels like everything is hopeless!" Daniel said, "Hope will find a way to defeat despair!" Sam looked outside the janitor's closet, and saw Matt! Sam said, "We need a plan to turn Matt back to normal!" Jay pointed to Chris and said, "We will use Chris as bait!" Chris walked out of the janitor's closet, and threw a cream pie at Matt! The cream pie hits Matt in the chest. Sam runs out of the janitor's closet, and tackled Matt in to the ground. Sam held Matt on the ground. Matt threw Sam off of him. Peter tackled Matt in to the ground, and held him down. Matt was struggling in Peter's grip. Jay grabbed the electric collar out of Tom's hand, and tossed it to Peter. Peter caught the electric collar, and wrapped it around Matt's neck. Quentin pressed the button and electrocuted Matt, multiple times! Matt's eyes turned back to normal, as he laid on the ground. Peter got up from the ground, and wiped the dust off of his clothes. Matt gets up and rubbed his head! Joey hugged Matt and said, "He's back to normal!" Matt said, "What happened!" Tom said, "Sally and Fiona brainwashed you, and your actions made you kill Anha!" Matt broke down in tears and cried! Joey wiped away Matt's tears and said, "It's not your fault, Sally wanted hope to be destroyed!" Sally spun in the headmaster's chair, and threw a stack of books at Fiona. Sally growled and said, "Why does hope keep getting in the way of my plans?" Fiona said, "The students are better, and more talented than us!" Sally kicked Fiona in the chest and said, "Despair never gives up! The students aren't better than us" Sally pressed a button and a giant robot smashed through the wall in to the hallway. Sally said, "Lets see the students try to defeat the giant robot." The giant robot smashed through the school's hallway as he said, "Beep, beep, beep, beep!" Harry walked in to the hallway, and threw a tub of ice cream at the giant robot. The giant robot beeped, and chased Harry down the hallway. Harry ran down the hallway, while the giant robot shot missiles at him. Harry dodged the missiles, and tore the water fountain out of the ground. Harry threw the water fountain at the giant robot. The giant robot grabbed the water fountain and smashed it to pieces. The giant robot shot a grappling hook at Harry. The grappling hook wrapped around Harry and pulled him in to the giant robot's hand. The giant robot petted Harry with his hand and said, "Harry, your life will be over soon, Despair will win, beep beep beep beep!" The giant robot picked Harry up by his neck. Harry struggled in his grip! The giant robot threw Harry in to the locker. Harry laid on the ground! The giant robot stepped on Harry's back! Harry screamed in pain, as blood poured on to the ground. Harry took out a nail from his pocket, and stabbed it in to the giant robot's leg. The giant robot stumbled backwards, as Harry used his strength to get up from the ground. Harry pushed the giant robot in to the wall. The giant robot kicked Harry in to the locker. Harry laid against the locker! The giant robot tackled Harry in to the ground, and punched him in the face. Harry growled, and held the giant robot's hand back! Harry pushed the giant robot off of him with his other hand. Harry got up from the ground! The giant robot launched a energy wave out of its body! Harry rolled on the ground, and laid against the wall. The giant robot picked up Harry and smashed him in to the locker. Harry laid on the ground! Spikes popped out of the giant robot's legs!The giant robot stepped on Harry's back! Blood poured out of Harry's body! The other students were terrified in horror. The giant robot patrolled the hallway. Daniel and Peter looked out in to the hallway, and saw the giant robot. Daniel said, "We need a plan to get to the headmaster's office, and take down Sally and Fiona!" Peter said,

"We work better as a team, let me call over the other students" Peter walks out in to the hallway, while the giant robot isn't looking. Peter flaps his arms like a bird! Peter said, "Tweet tweet tweet tweet!" The other students saw Peter, and walked out of the janitor's closet to his location. Tony walked out of his locker, and toward Peter. Peter said, "Everyone is together, lets think of a plan!" Daniel said, "We need a student to distract the giant robot, while the rest of us hunt down Sally and Fiona." Chris said, "We could volunteer Joey as the distraction!" Abby said, "The giant robot is scary, and I don't want him to mess up Joey's hair. His hair is so soft, and Joey is the nicest student that I know." Quentin hugs Joey and said, "I won't let the giant robot smash him in to the ground, Joey is my best friend." Quentin squeezes Joey tightly. Joey coughs and said, "Quentin, I can't breathe, you're squeezing me too

tight!" Quentin said, "You're my best friend though!" Peter grabbed Quentin by his shirt collar, and dragged him backwards! Joey said, "Thanks Peter, you're the best!" Peter said, "No problem, Joey!" Abby hugged Peter and said, "Peter, you're a life saver." Peter said, "Thanks Abby!" Quentin leans against the wall! Peter said, "Anyone else have a good idea?" Noah said, "One of my friends, Aaron, can distract the giant robot for us!" Noah whistles outside the room in to the hallway. Aaron walked through the hallway, and pushes the giant robot in to the lockers. The giant robot falls on the ground, and smashes the water fountain. Aaron walked in to the men's bathroom. Aaron tapped Noah on the shoulder. Noah said, "He can distract the giant robot for us, while we take down Sally and Fiona." Peter smiled and said, "Sounds like the perfect plan!" Peter and Daniel gathered the other students in

a group. Aaron marched in the front of the other students with Daniel and Peter. Aaron threw a cream pie at the giant robot to distract him, while the other students ran through the hallway to the headmaster's office. The giant robot saw the other students, and chased after them. Bob said, "The giant robot is chasing us, we need to run faster." Daniel said, "Good idea, Bob!" The other students ran faster to the headmaster's office, while Aaron stood in front of the giant robot, and hit him with apples, to slow him down. The giant robot swatted Aaron away with his hand, and launched a rope at Bob. The rope wrapped around Bob, as he fell on the ground. The giant robot walked closer to Bob. Peter looked back, and saw that Bob fell in the hallway. Daniel said, "Peter, keep your eye on the objective!" Peter nodded and continued running. Abby said, "I am not leaving a student behind, Daniel." Daniel said, "It is too dangerous, Abby!" Abby said, "I know that it is dangerous, but I am willing to risk my life." Abby and Joey hugged each other. Abby ran in front of Bob, and tried to untie the rope around him. The giant robot walked toward Abby, and grabbed her with his hand." Aaron walked toward the giant robot. The giant robot punched Aaron in to the wall. Aaron rubbed his head! The giant robot shot a missile at Bob. Bob smashed in to the lockers and laid next to the lockers, with blood on the ground. The giant robot kicked Bob in to the lockers with his foot. Bob laid on the ground. The giant robot sharpened the spikes on his foot, and stepped on Bob's chest. Blood poured on to the ground, as Bob's body laid on the ground. Abby was terrified in horror! The giant robot grabbed Abby by her neck, and smashed her in to the locker. Blood poured on to the ground, as she laid next to the wall. The giant robot took out his spiked sword, and stabbed Abby in the chest. A puddle of blood formed under her body. Aaron walked toward the giant robot with his flaming sword, and swung it at the giant robot. The spiked sword was destroyed by the flaming sword! Aaron growled and shot the giant robot with a pie launcher. The giant robot stumbled on to the ground, and exploded. Body parts flew everywhere in the debris! Joey and the other students saw the chaos behind them, as they wiped the tears out of their eyes. They ran toward the headmaster's office. Sally growled and threw knifes at the wall, while Fiona dodged them. Sally said, "I hate hope so much, seeing our work fall apart fills me with so much despair." Fiona said, "That's how life works, it would be boring if despair controlled the world. Hope and Despair keeps everything balanced." Sally said, "Hope and Despair are two sides of the same coin!" Daniel kicked down the

headmaster's door. Daniel and the rest of the students walked in to the headmaster's office. Peter said, "You lost, Sally and Fiona! We have you outnumbered!" Sally laughed and said, "Outnumbered, you make me laugh! We are the queens of despair, and all of you have fallen in to our trap." Fiona pressed a button on the wall, and a energy shield formed around the students. Sally said, "Get cozy, we want to have some fun with you!" Fiona grabbed a rope and threw it around Gwen. Sally pulled Gwen closer to her. Sally brushed Gwen with her hand. Sally said, "Your hair is so shiny and wonderful, too bad that we have to cut it off." Sally grinned, as she took out a razor out of her bag. Sally turned on the razor, and shaved all of Gwen's hair off of her head. The students were horrified as hair flew everywhere, and on to the ground. Sally gave Gwen a mirror! Gwen screamed in horror, as she saw herself in

the mirror. Sally said, "We're not done yet!" Fiona gave a chainsaw to Sally! Sally turned on the chainsaw, and pushed it through Gwen's chest! Blood flew everywhere, and Gwen's body laid on the ground. Peter growled and shouted," NOOOOOOOOOOOOOOOOOO, she didn't deserve to die, both of you are monsters!" Sam put his hand on Peter's shoulder and said, "Everything will be fine!" Sally said, "Awwwwwww, the students are upset at us for killing their friend!" Tony picked up Matt's knife and stabbed through the energy shield. Tony tackled Fiona in to the wall. Fiona kicked Tony in the chest. Fiona grabbed Tony's arm. Tony backflips and kicked Fiona in the face. Tony grabbed Fiona's arm, and stabbed her in the neck with the knife. Tony roundhouse kicked Fiona in the chest. Fiona smashed in to the wall. Tony punched Fiona in the face. Blood poured on the ground. Fiona got up from the ground, and grabbed Tony by his neck. Fiona body slammed Tony in to the ground. Tony got up from the ground, and tackled Fiona in to the wall. Tony picked up Fiona by her neck, and slammed her in to the ground. Fiona stabbed her knife in to Tony's arm! Blood poured out on to Fiona's chest, while Tony choked Fiona. Tony squeezed Fiona's neck, while she was coughing! Tony roundhouse kicked Fiona in the face. Fiona stumbled backwards! Tony put the knife in his pocket, while he walked over and picked up the chainsaw. Tony stepped on Fiona's legs to hold her down. Tony started up the chainsaw and stabbed it in to Fiona's chest. Blood poured out of her body, as she laid on the ground. Tony wiped the blood off of his shoes, as Sally growled at him. Sally said, "Hope is so annoying, despair will not give up!" Tony said, "You killed our friends, your reign of terror will be over!" Sally said, "Despair will consume your soul!" Sally kicked Tony in the chest, and stepped on his back. Sally whacked Tony in the back, multiple times with the electric baton. The electric baton electrocuted Tony, while he screamed in pain. Sally picked up Tony's body, and smashed him through the headmaster's desk. Tony got up from the ground! Sally threw throwing knifes at Tony. The throwing knifes sliced through Tony's body, as blood leaked on the ground. Tony threw a water fountain at Sally. Sally dodged the water fountain, as it smashed against the wall. Sally sped in to Tony, and smashed him in to the wall. The wall made a dent, and the shotput ball machine activated. The shotput ball machine dropped a shotput ball on Tony's foot. Tony screamed in pain! Tony limped toward Sally. Tony swung his arm at Sally. Sally grabbed Tony's arm, and kicked him in the chest. Sally grabbed her knife, and stabbed Tony in the neck. Sally picked up the chainsaw! Sally stabbed the chainsaw through Tony's body. Blood flew everywhere, while Tony's body laid on the ground. Peter growled at Sally, as she put the chainsaw on to the ground. Sally said, "Awwww, did I make you mad for killing your friend!" Peter growled and said, "You are a monster, Tony was our best friend." Peter walked closer to Sally, and picked up a knife from the ground. Peter sped in to Sally! Sally swung her arm at Peter! Peter grabbed her arm, and threw her at the wall. Peter flipped in the air, and did a spinning roundhouse kick in to Sally's chest. Sally smashed in to the bookshelf, and laid against the wall. Peter grabbed Sally by her neck, and body slammed her in to the ground. Sally laid on the ground, while Peter stepped on her back to hold her down. Peter bent down and stabbed the knife in to Sally's neck. Blood poured on to the ground. Sally grabbed on to a table leg to help herself

up. Sally got up from the ground! Peter sped in to Sally, and tackled her in to the wall. Peter punched Sally in the face! Peter growled and said, "You are a monster for killing several of our friends, you deserve to die." Sally said, "That's how despair works! It consumes your soul, when one drop of blood pours on to the ground." Sally kicked Peter in the chest. Peter slid backwards! Sally threw throwing knives at Peter! Peter flipped in the air, and dodged them. Peter landed on the ground! Peter sped in to Sally, and grabbed her neck. Peter body slammed Sally in to the ground. Sally got up from the ground. Peter sped in to Sally, and kicked her in the chest. Sally slid next to the wall. Peter threw his rope at Sally. The rope twisted around Sally! Peter pulled on the rope, and dragged Sally closer to him. Sally swung her arm at Peter. Peter grabbed Sally's arm, and threw her at the wall. Sally laid against

the wall. Peter picked Sally up by her neck and stabbed the knife in to her chest! Blood splashed on to the ground, as Peter threw Sally on to the ground. Peter said, "Your reign of terror is over, Sally!" Peter put the knife on the desk, that was next to him. Peter picked up the shotput ball from the ground, and smashed it on top of Sally's head, multiple times as blood splashed on to the ground. Sally's body laid on the ground! Peter set the shotput ball on to the ground, and picked up a towel from the headmaster's desk. Peter wiped the blood off of his body with a towel. The school's alarm system went off! Pine Cone Academy Alarm System said, "Warning! Automatic Self Destruction System has activated, all students must get out of the blast radius immediately." Beeping goes off in the background, as the energy shield dropped around the other students. Aaron walked in to the

headmaster's room, and helped the students get out of the blast radius. Daniel and Peter ran out of the headmaster's room, with the other students behind them. The headmaster's room exploded, as the students dived for cover in the men's bathroom. Dust and debris covered the hallway, and filled the air with dust particles. The air returns to normal, while Daniel and Peter walked in to the hallway to check out the chaos. Daniel and Peter were terrified in horror from all of the debris. Peter said, "It was a tough battle, but we have defeated Sally and Fiona." Daniel said, "Yep, the students worked together as a team." Peter and Daniel hugged each other, while the other students celebrated by eating ice cream. The storm of despair has been defeated, and the students have restored hope in the environment of Pine Cone Academy.

ABOUT THE AUTHOR

Josh Zimmer is an crazy individual with an extreme imagination. He loves to have fun by listening to music, writing stories, and playing video games of various genres such as platforming, multiplayer online games, role playing games, and sports games. His favorite technology brands are Nintendo and Microsoft. They are wonderful role models for the industry. He commands an army of cats to his will with hugs, love, and snacks. He makes the cats purr and meow with happiness.

www.ingramcontent.com/pod-product-compliance
Lightning Source LLC
Chambersburg PA
CBHW060620310726
48982CB00003B/620

* 9 7 8 0 5 7 8 5 8 2 4 5 0 *